D
E

F

I

J

N

O

P

S

T

X

Y

Z

Sophie

S O P H I E

Discovers Synchronized Swimming

S Y N C H R O N I Z E D

S W I M M I N G

Illustrations by Robert Noreika

ISBN 978-0983-12111

For Children With Love
P.O. Box 1552
Farmington, Connecticut 06034

Visit our website www.forchildrenwithlove.com

Printed in Singapore by Tien Wah Press (Pte) Limited, First Printing, May 2012
16 15 14 13 12 • 5 4 3 2 1

Sophie

S O P H I E

Discovers Synchronized Swimming

Author, Catherine Gibson

Illustrator, Robert Noreika

For Children With Love Publications
Farmington, Connecticut
Visit our website www.forchildrenwithlove.com

A portion of the proceeds from each book sold is donated to the For Children With Love Foundation which supports local children's causes. visit www.forchildrenwithlove.com

It was a rainy Thursday afternoon. Sophie had finished her homework and began practicing ballet positions at the barre in her bedroom. Sophie loved ballet. She would twirl around for hours.

While Sophie was stretching on the floor, she noticed the light on her computer blinking on and off. She walked over to the computer to see who had sent her a message. It was from her cousin, Gilly. It read, "Sophie, would you like to come to my swim meet tomorrow at three o'clock?" Sophie replied, "I would love to see your swim meet. Let me ask my mom and I will get back to you soon."

Light

Read

Swim

Tomorrow

Sophie noticed the light on her bedroom wall blinking. Because Sophie was deaf, her mother would blink the lights as a signal to Sophie if they were not in the same room. This time it meant that it was time for dinner. Sophie skipped and pirouetted to the dinner table. Her mother signed to her, "What is all of the excitement?"

Sophie signed back, "Gilly invited me to her swim meet tomorrow at three o'clock. Can I go? Can I, please?" signed Sophie. Her mom signed back, "It sounds like a lot of fun and of course you can go."

Because

Deaf

Can

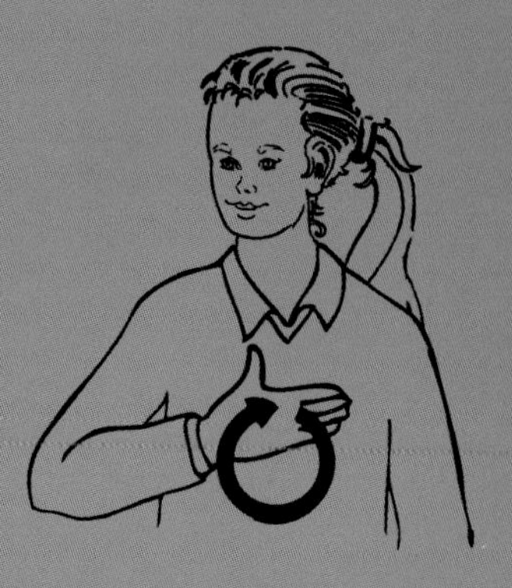
Please

Sophie couldn't wait to send a message back to her cousin telling her that she could go to the pool and watch Gilly compete. The computer was Sophie's best way to communicate with others when they weren't together. Gilly knew some sign language, but not enough to understand everything Sophie said.

The next day Sophie and her mother arrived at the pool and sat with Gilly's mom. Sophie had taken lessons as a little girl and had become an excellent swimmer. She was very excited, not knowing what to expect at the competition.

Compete

Together

Sign Language

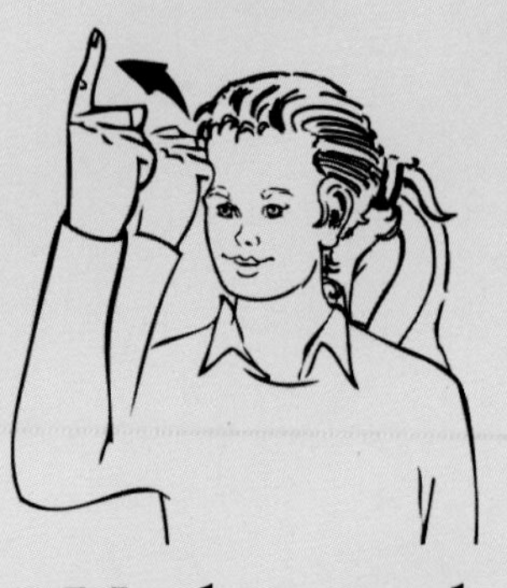

Understand

There were girls kicking on the side of the pool, some practicing dives and others swimming underwater. There were also girls forming circles in the pool, making movements like dancers in the water. They were all wearing matching, blue bathing suits with white caps on their heads. "Mom, what are those girls doing?" signed Sophie. "I'm not sure," her mother signed, shrugging her shoulders.

There were flags flying in the pool area and there was enthusiasm all around, as the crowd clapped and cheered. Sophie watched, wide-eyed.

Kicking

Practicing

Wearing

Blue

Gilly walked out for her race. A flag came down for the race to begin; it was the free-style. Gilly swam her hardest. Her hand was the first to touch the pool wall; she turned to look at Sophie. Sophie waved to Gilly, gave her a thumbs up and signed, "Good! Good!" Gilly gave her a thumbs up back, laughed and signed, "Thank you!"

Gilly's race was the last one of the competition. Next, a group of girls came out. They were also wearing matching bathing suits. They were not competing against each other in a race; they were performing together. Gilly quickly jumped into the pool to join them. Sophie signed to her mom, asking again, "What are they going to do?" Her mother shook her head and signed, "Let's watch and see."

Good

Thank You

Girl

Performing

Sophie's mom asked Gilly's mother what the girls were going to do. Gilly's mother replied that they were synchronized swimmers, who are like dancers in water. Sophie's mom signed to Sophie and fingerspelled, "s-y-n-c-h-r-o-n-i-z-e-d s-w-i-m-m-e-r-s." With a twinkle in her eye, Sophie watched as they performed. The dancers' legs would come up out of the water, one leg at a time. They would separate into groups, forming different shapes in the water, their heads turning in the same direction at the same time. The girls looked like graceful swans. They were spinning and twirling in the water!

Fingerspell

Water

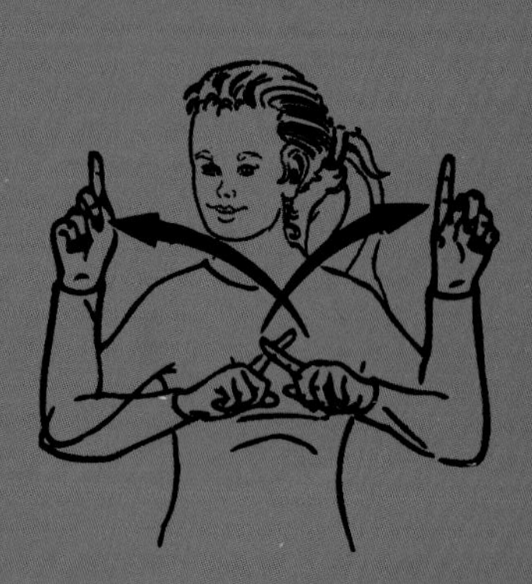

Different

Same

It was hard to believe that they were not on a dance floor. They were doing something Sophie had never seen before in the water. Sophie quietly stood up, signing the word "Love," with her arms across her chest. She looked over at her mom and signed, "Beautiful!"

Traveling home, Sophie signed to her mother, "Mom, I want to learn to dance in the water." Her mother signed back that a person not only needs to be a very strong swimmer, like Sophie had become, but it also takes a lot of time and training to learn how to synchronize swim. Her mother suggested that they ask Gilly if she would be willing to work with Sophie.

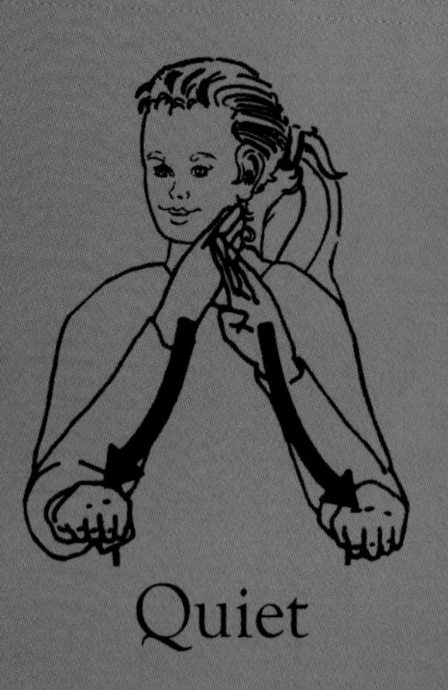

Quiet

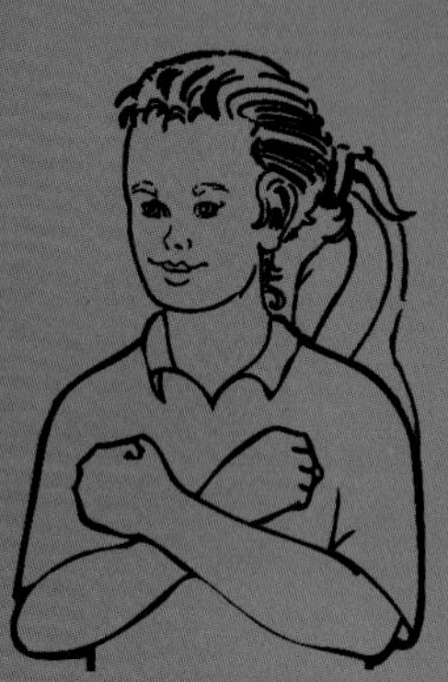

Love

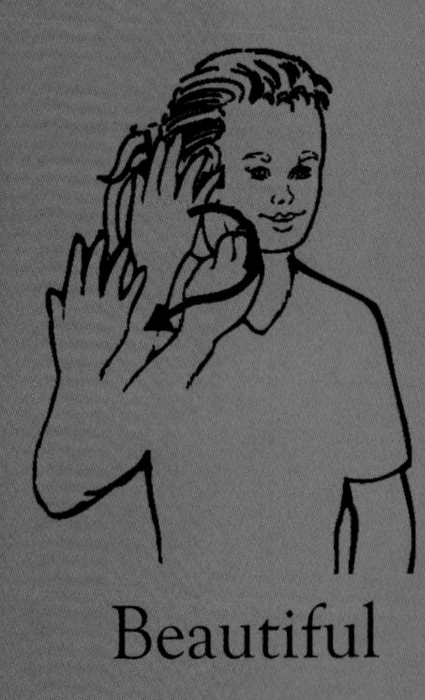

Beautiful

Learn

The following day, they met Gilly at the pool. Gilly was very excited to know that Sophie wanted to become involved in synchronized swimming and told her she would be happy to help her.

The girls began to meet at the pool each day. They spent many hours practicing. Gilly showed Sophie how, by simply using tiny movements of her hands below the water, she could move into different positions more easily. Gilly would have her turn in a circle or go forward and backward, all without seeming to move any part of her body. They practiced floating into different positions, moving their legs and arms apart and together, making shapes and figures to the music like a kaleidoscope that is ever-changing.

Excite

Want

Happy

Help

Soon it was time to add the music; Gilly played it loudly. There were speakers underwater, so that when the swimmers performed, they were able to hear the beat. To Sophie's amazement, she was able to feel the music's vibrations. She was able to keep the movements the same as her cousin's. Weeks went by and Sophie would go to the pool each day to practice. The other swimmers were also there practicing.

On this particular day, Gilly asked the girls if Sophie could swim with them. She explained that Sophie was deaf, but that she was able to feel the vibrations in the water, she was a strong swimmer and she had been practicing their routine. The girls looked at each other, shook their heads no and walked away. They were afraid that because Sophie was deaf and could not hear the music, she would not be able to keep up with them and she would ruin their routine.

Music

Loudly

Amazement

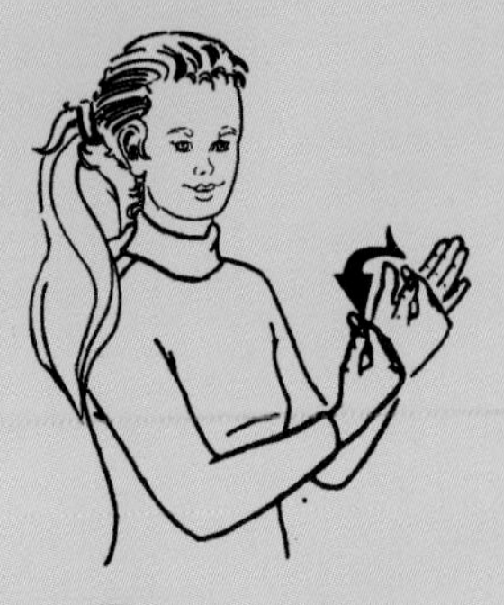

Routine

Sophie looked at her cousin with tears in her eyes. She put her head down so the girls wouldn't see how sad she felt. Gilly reached for Sophie's hand and signed, "Sorry." Sophie signed back, "Thank you!" And together, they walked home hand in hand.

A month went by and the same girls were in a circle watching Sophie practice in the pool. One of the girls turned to the others and said, "Sophie is a very good swimmer, let's have her practice with us." Another said, "No, she can't hear us!" As the girls stood mumbling to one another Gilly went over to them and firmly said, "You are not being nice to Sophie. Say you're sorry! This is the sign to say you're sorry. Give her a chance!"

The girls looked at one another, feeling badly about how they had treated her. One by one, the girls jumped into the pool. "Sorry!" "Sorry!" "Sorry!" they each signed to Sophie. Gilly tapped Sophie on the shoulder and signed, "Let's dance with the others in the water." Sophie's mom was sitting at the side of the pool. She slowly stood up and proudly watched Sophie jump into the water to perform the routine in the pool with the other swimmers.

Gilly started the music, and signed to Sophie, "Dance! Dance! Dance!" and that Sophie did!

Feeling

Jumped

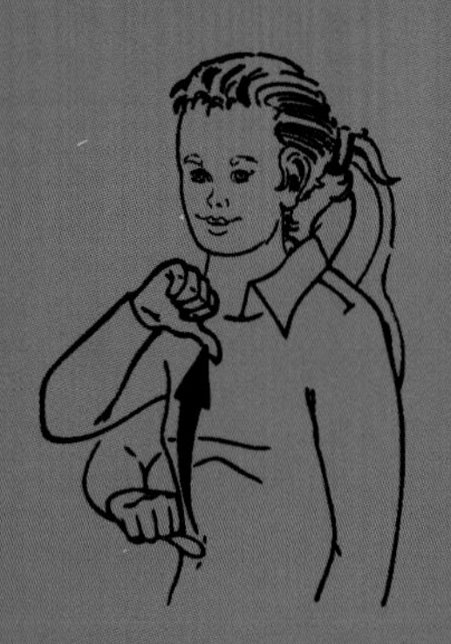

Proudly

Dance

Her legs came out of the water one at a time, kicking and spinning. Sophie was floating on her back as if someone was holding her. She turned her head from side to side, in sync with the other swimmers. Her mother was standing, grinning from ear to ear as the crowd watched and cheered!

At the end of the routine, the girls formed a circle creating the look of a beautiful flower.

Mother

Standing

Watched

Flower

In the middle was a special place for only one swimmer. The girls chose Sophie! With their arms positioned toward her in the center, Sophie came out of the water and it looked as though she was moving in slow motion.

The water glistened off her body, Sophie looked straight into her mother's proud eyes and signed, "I love you!" Her mom signed back, "I love you, too!"

Chose

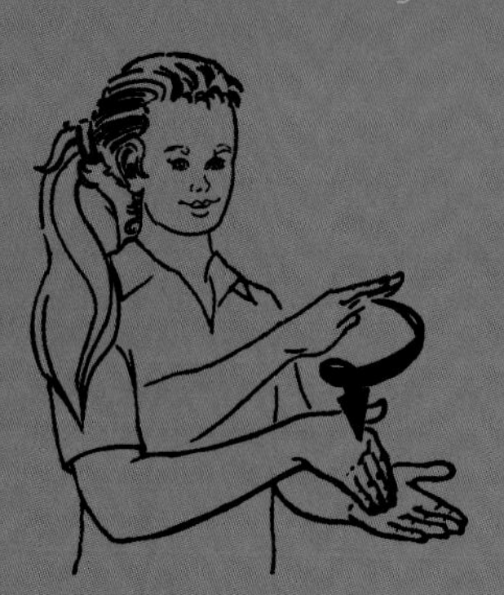

Center

Slow

I love you

Sophie

S O P H I E

Discovers Synchronized Swimming

Author

Author Bio

Author Catherine Czerwinski Gibson's first book, *Through Sophie's Eyes,* was published in 2009, the winner of an Independent Book Publisher's Award and a Mom's Choice Award. In 2011, Cathy was named Woman of the Year, by the National Association of Professional Women. She also published her second book, titled *Coach Bob & Me*, about the friendship between a boy who is a loner and an inspirational coach who is confined to a wheelchair.

Sophie Discovers Synchronized Swimming is the sequel to her first Sophie book. A deaf friend, who competed to become a national champion synchronized swimmer, inspired Cathy to write this story.

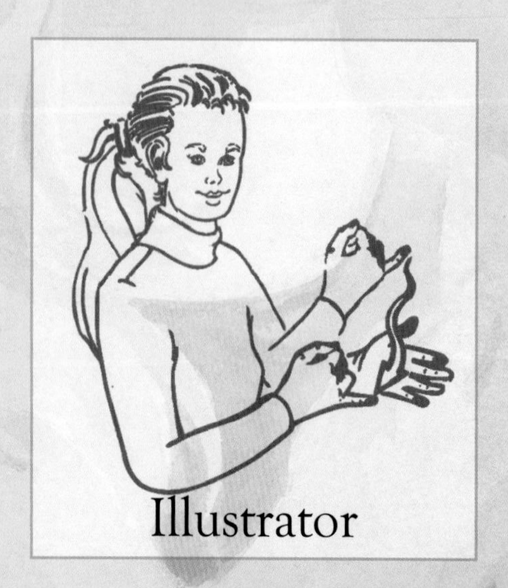
Illustrator

Illustrator Bio

Robert Noreika is a watercolorist who attended the Paier College of Art in Hamden, Connecticut. He has an art studio in the Arts Center in Avon, Connecticut. He lives with his wife Chris and daughter, Sarah. This is the twelfth book he has illustrated.

Thank You

To Scott Sierakowski
for the computer magic he performs
turning the pictures and words of my stories into pages.

To Debbie Andrews
graphic designer, editor and friend
who helps me turn those pages into books.

Public awareness of those with life challenges has become a necessary and important issue in today's world. It is that message which Cathy conveys in her thoughtful stories of children with special gifts who are accepted for their individual strengths and winning personalities.

www.forchildrenwithlove.com

Cathy Gibson is the recipient of the Mom's Choice Award and the Independent Book Publisher's Award for her first book, *Through Sophie's Eyes*. In 2011, Cathy was honored as "Woman of the Year" by The National Association of Professional Women.

Children's books with a positive message of giving, understanding and acceptance

For more information and news please visit our website
www.forchildrenwithlove.com

To Aryanna –

follow your dreams! ♡

xo...

:) Catherine [illegible]

A
B
C
G
H
K
L
M
Q
R
U
V
W